THE BOY WHO SANG THE BIRDS

~

THE BOY WHO SANG THE BIRDS

by John Weston

Drawings by Donna Diamond

CHARLES SCRIBNER'S SONS ~ NEW YORK

This book published simultaneously in the
United States of America and in Canada —

Printed in the United States of America
Library of Congress Catalog Card Number 75-27706
1 3 5 7 9 11 13 15 17 19 MD/C 20 18 16 14 12 10 8 6 4 2
ISBN 0-684-14534-0

~ *To honor life in nature*

Dorkle lived with Tobe beyond the great creek, and farther.

Tobe's cabin, leaning to one side like a tired horse, stood in the paw of the peaked blue mountain. Behind it the granite rocks tumbled upward. Before it, the field sloped toward a damp pasture.

It had not always been so—that Dorkle lived with Tobe. Or that Tobe himself lived without parents in the leaning cabin.

Dorkle was discovered in a tree.

One warm day, while sharing a shaft of sunlight and a plug of tobacco on the store porch in Charley Crossing, three old men looked up to see the willow that grew there shaking furiously as if a wind had hold of it.

"Ah, ha!" said one old man. "There's a crow in the tree." He pointed with his stick.

"Wrong," said the second old man. "I say it's a goat."

"Or a mountain lion," said the third, squinting.

The tree continued to shake. It gathered its long branches together like a girl drying her hair and shivering. The old men continued to argue. The sunlight moved.

In a while, slithering down one of the slender branches came a plain boy, barefooted, with matty hair the color of yellow squash, and viola-blue eyes. Sitting back, the three old men stamped their shoes and said, "Pooh! It's only a boy," and went on to other subjects.

But no one knew what to make of this boy who sat thereafter on the porch steps watching people come to buy groceries and go.

He didn't belong to anybody in Charley Crossing because a count was taken and there were no missing boys. Some of the spotted dogs of the village, of which there were many, came by and licked his hand or sat a few minutes on the step beside him and hung out their tongues and allowed their heads to be touched.

"What should be done with him?" the people said. They stood inside the store and looked out at the back of his head. Or they gathered in the road and looked at his round eyes. The word, as if it had wings, flew up and down the valley and people came walking in the dust or riding in their dusty vehicles. Inside the store they bought things they hadn't planned to buy and didn't need and said, "Who's going to see after him?"

"I don't want no boy that can't talk," one woman said.

"Nor I," said another. The people nodded.

The boy could talk, in a way. It was only that his words came out in an order that made no sense to the people of Charley Crossing. "Where you from?" they asked him.

And he answered, "Trees, sky the yellow over, *dorkle*."

"Eh?" they said. "Where? Who's your folks?"

"Fee the green, *dorkle*. Cats." He blinked his viola-blue eyes.

The *dorkle*-sound he made was something like a blackbird makes, sparkling and far-singing, crackling, bright, and clear like water.

"Impudent, if you ask me," a very pretty lady said. She bought a length of green cloth and when passing the boy, as she must to descend the steps, held her skirt in one hand.

"And raggedy," said another.

"We ought to hold a meeting," Cooney Mede said to his passel of fellow loafers. They leaned on the porch posts, discussing the boy as if he were a package.

"Yeh," Mars Krookford said. "Or ask old lady Bonihander. Witches is supposed to know everything."

Cooney Mede and the others laughed.

Finally, the people went home, even the old men, whom the sun deserted.

In the store, the fellow called Tobe put away his broom. He also watched the boy's back as he sat on the steps and made sounds to a dog. The dog tipped his head this way, then that. "Who is he?" Tobe asked the storekeeper.

"Beats me." They stood in the darkening building watching the strange boy. "Well, I have to close up. And you better be getting on home. You have a long ways before full dark."

"It doesn't matter when I get home. There's nobody to say."

The storekeeper paused before turning out the last light. He saw Tobe standing there looking dark and scowling, working the muscles of his jaw. "You could take him with you. To your place."

"I don't need anybody," Tobe said.

"He'd be company. Least till his people come and find him."

"I don't need company."

Mr. Stooper finished pulling the shades down inside his windows and covering up things for the night. "He's not an awful lot younger'n you."

"Ha. How old you figure he is?"

"I don't know. Eight, maybe?"

Tobe put his hands in the back pockets of his jeans. On his feet he wore cowboy boots with run-over heels. He rocked back and forth on them. "I'm twice as old as that. Nearly."

"Well," the storekeeper said.

"What do I need with a little kid?"

"Suit yourself. Don't forget your groceries."

Tobe, tall for his age, and growing heavy in the shoulders, stopped on the porch and looked from the willow tree down to the matted yellow head. "You come along with me," he said. "If you want to."

"Vines? Barrels around inside. For cracks."

"I don't know. Come on—we have a long walk ahead."

"*Dorkle,*" the boy said. He walked along beside Tobe, holding up his overalls with one hand, except when he forgot to and then had to grab them at the last second and stop and haul them up again.

"Why are you so raggedy?" Tobe asked. He looked straight ahead down the road.

The boy ran, stirring the dust with his feet, and said, "Gum the far under, pines."

"You have to keep up," Tobe said. "I can't wait around till kingdom come for you to catch up."

The birds, settling for the night into the cottonwoods along the road, seemed to Tobe to be going about it in an unnecessarily loud way. Behind the tall mountain, now black like a peaked hat, the sky turned pale as beaten brass.

"I live back yonder," Tobe said. "Back at the foot of the mountain. It'll be dark long before we get there." He looked toward the inky cone and waited until he heard the scramble of the boy's feet and overalls beside him. He sighed. "At this rate, it'll be morning."

"Watermelon after, up the rings and fire."

"I don't know about that," Tobe said. And then after a while he added, "You'll have to learn to talk like anybody else if we're going to get along."

"*Dorkle?*"

"Yeh. Come on." Tobe turned off the main road down a long straight lane lined with cottonwoods that linked their branches together overhead. Their trunks stood thick and pale in the last light, but it was dark under their arch. "You afraid of the dark?" Tobe asked. "Isn't anything to be afraid of in it. I walk around in it all the time. I even live in it sometimes, if I want to." He waited until he heard the soft scrabbling beside him.

"I do whatever I want," Tobe said. "Mostly."

"Cake, sky the rocks," panted the voice. "Rumbles."

"I can take care of myself. I've been doing it, and I can keep on. A year, I've been doing it, since my father died and my mother . . . left."

He helped the boy over a stile at the end of the lane. It was brighter there. Before them lay the wide pale body of the great creek. "It's dry now," Tobe said, "but when it storms. . . ." They walked across the sand.

"Anyway, about six months after he died, one day my mother said we were going away to live with a man from St. Johns—that's down the road I don't know how many miles. 'I'm not,' I said. And she said I had to and I said I wouldn't. I packed a sack and hid out in the rocks and finally they went away."

"Fry the if, and, willows blue."

"Which was just fine with me. I said 'I don't need anybody,' and I don't. Come on now, we have a long way yet."

The night fell down around them. Tobe followed the double-track road that wound among dark humps of elderberry bushes or ran clear and pale across open spaces. A half-moon, already far up in the sky, sent down light.

"Don't you have a name?" Tobe asked the puffing form that ran sometimes beside him, sometimes behind.

"Far the well. Dandelions. Soup."

An owl hooted twice ahead of them. When they walked under his tree he flew away fast across the moon. From another direction they heard a whippoorwill. He repeated his three tones, hollow-sounding like notes from a wooden flute.

"I'm going to call you Dorkle, then."

"*Dorkle!*"

"Yeh. You can't just go along without a name. People can't. Animals—they don't have to have names if they don't want to. Someday, I'm going to have lots of animals. Cattle. And a horse." He shifted the bags in his arms and waited until Dorkle reached his side.

"Right now, I don't have many animals.

Two goats. Cat. One old hen about to croak and an old cow that mostly just lies around."

"In the cake. Mumble." The voice began to sound run-down and tired.

In another mile, through a wooden gate that creaked open and sagged against the ground, they came to the last turn in the road.

"There," Tobe said, stopping. "Can you see it?"

Even in the near-dark he could see how the house sagged away to one side. And he could see the outline of the barn and the skeleton of the windmill rising, black and silver.

Dorkle seemed to pick up a little energy. He ran ahead and was waiting by the next gate, tugging at it, when Tobe got there.

They went into the house. Tobe lighted a lamp and the cat came out from behind the cold stove blinking.

"It may not be the best," Tobe said, "but it's

all I need." He removed a package of beans and one of dried fruit from his bags.

"Dog besides, a fine pink. Cookies." Dorkle was bending down touching the top of the cat's head. She closed her eyes and stretched up her neck.

"No, that's not a dog. I just call her Cat. They left her here, too. And that old brown cow everybody thought was about to die. Only she hasn't yet."

The next time he looked, Dorkle was sitting on the floor with his feet out in front and the cat sprawled across his lap like a fur rug. One of them was making a contented noise.

"I work for Mr. Stooper at the store, two, sometimes three days a week. And I've got that old hen—too old to lay anymore. Everybody said I couldn't just stay out here, but I'm doing it. I've been doing it."

Not hearing any response, he looked again

at the cat and the boy. "You asleep?"

"Mumbles, pie . . . *dorkle,*" he thought he heard the boy say.

"I don't know what I'm supposed to do with you, though." Tobe pulled a blanket off his bed and wrapped it around the boy. The viola-colored eyes were closed. His hair was just about the color of one of Cat's three colors. She curled up at his feet.

"A cat, a sick hen, an old broken-down cow, two worthless goats," Tobe said. "And now you. I must be crazy."

He sat a time longer in the yellow light of the lamp with his boots out in front and his hands behind his head. Outside he heard the running, garbling cry of a coyote far back in the hills ; it sounded like a weeping woman.

That's how Dorkle came to be discovered and to live with Tobe in the leaning cabin beyond the wide creek. The people of Charley Crossing discussed them now and then, supposing they would come to no good end, but—like the three old men on the porch—they soon turned to other matters.

One of the new arguments among the three old men warming in the sun had to do with birds.

"There's more of them than ever," one said.

"No, there ain't," said the second.

"Always is, come fall," said the third. "They're fixing to migrate. Going this way and that."

"There's more, I tell you," said the first. "Screechin' and cheepin'."

"I don't hear nothing."

"Well *look,* then. Look there in the willow tree." The old man stamped his shoe and stick.

The mornings opened warm and brilliant with sun. The people came to the store with empty baskets and left with full ones. By afternoon, white clouds and gray ones rose heavy and full, looked over the mountains, then withdrew. The birds gathered nervously in the trees.

Tobe hoed and watered his vegetable garden on the days when he did not walk to Charley Crossing to work for the storekeeper, keeping his summer squash picked and bearing, measuring the size of his winter squash, imagining what the carrots and turnips and potatoes were doing underground. Or he watched his apples reddening on his tree. Sometimes he took a board off the barn and nailed it over a crack in the leaning cabin. Sometimes he looked at his field and said, "I'm going to have red cattle one of these days. Then this here will be a true ranch." He'd lift up and re-set his hat and lean on his hoe.

"Pears, bubble the triangles," Dorkle said, pausing in his flight from one place to another.

Tobe had awakened, the first morning Dorkle lived there, to the faint groaning of the old brown cow in the barn. When he went out, he found the boy pushing at her from behind, trying to get her up and into the sunlight.

"Hey," he said. "You can't make that old cow move if she doesn't want to."

The boy looked up with his wide round eyes. Then he looked again at the cow, who was watching him tiredly. He gave her a sound kick in the rear with his bare foot, then hobbled out the barn door. In a minute, the old cow groaned once more but got up, ringing her solemn bell, and followed him into the yard.

By then he was squatting in front of the chicken coop looking eye-to-eye with the sickly hen. She had crept part way into the day with her rusty feathers ruffled and her head pulled back and with the blue-gray lids lifted halfway across her eyes. Her breast, like the prow of a canoe, bowed out bony and sharp. "*Dorkle!*" Dorkle said. "Up the sky, day. Gumdrops." The old hen squawked.

"She's not long for this world," Tobe said. "We might as well stew her."

"Peas," Dorkle said to the hen. "Green soup!" The chicken opened her eyes wider and looked from him to the grains of corn he dropped before her.

That day Dorkle made three trips down to

the meadow to bring the cow armloads of clover, some blossoming, some with bees, and a pocketful of green-and-yellow grasshoppers for the rusty hen.

The two goats watched him looking through the wire of their pen. Their eyes grew deep and yellow.

The following morning the cow walked out into the light without a kick and hung her head over the fence and made a round sound.

Shaking her feathers, the old hen was up when Dorkle arrived with her corn and bugs the second day. The third, she ran across her pen flapping her wings a little.

"Cake and rocks. Marbles!" Dorkle said the fourth morning, running into the house.

"What?" Tobe sat up in his bed. "What time is it?"

Dorkle held out his hand. There in the middle of it was a fat brown egg.

And that evening just before dark he came

crashing in. His feet danced, his hands racketed the pots and pans.

"What're you doing?" Tobe asked. "Come back here with those!"

The three-colored cat walked out from behind the stove looking interested.

"Bob, real," Dorkle said, clattering toward the door. "Far the green jagged apples up, limbs in the running dinner," which was a long sentence for him to say under the circumstances.

Tobe followed him across the yard. In her corral the brown cow stood anxiously, her bag heavy with milk. Dorkle dropped all the pots down beside her.

The days came and left. Sunrise and darkness. In the afternoons the clouds wandered up to look over the mountains. They stayed longer around the peak of the bald blue mountain behind Tobe's house, like a white muffler.

One day Tobe looked at Dorkle a long time and said, "You need a bath, I guess."

The boy turned his head and his eyes grew round.

"Well, don't look at me like that. Kids are supposed to have baths."

"*Dorkle?* Find the dark. Lunch."

"Not a regular bath with soap. I mean, we could go down to the swamp."

When Dorkle smiled the bottom row of his teeth stood up everywhichway, like tiny crooked tombstones.

"I dammed up a place," Tobe said. "It's for swimming. Sort of."

By then Dorkle's feet were moving although he was staying in about the same place.

They walked down the long pasture to the place Tobe meant, a shallow muddy pool in the shade of some cottonwoods where bright moss grew like long thick green hair. Tobe lay on the bank and watched Dorkle dunk his head under and laugh—a sound something like his name, tumbling and brookish.

Above them in the branches the birds gathered. The jays and the mockingbirds fought over imaginary territories. A woodpecker punctured a tree. In the highest limbs a pair of crows sat by an abandoned nest. From a long way off came the bawl of a calf. "Someday, I'm going to have red cattle," Tobe said with his hands behind his head. "Steers, a bull, cows. And horses."

"Bottles?" Dorkle said wetly. He waded closer with something squirming in his hand. "Rain below the purple."

"That's just a polliwog."

Dorkle looked at the fat black shape—a tiny whale. Nodding, he said, "The woggle."

"How'd you catch a polliwog in your bare hands?" He watched Dorkle bend over and put his hand in the water. The polliwog flipped his tail and disappeared. "How'd you do it?"

Dorkle smiled and splashed away across the pond. His hair had become mattier than ever.

The afternoon hummed with the sounds of bugs and grew warm until the gray-white clouds rolled up. Tobe dreamed of the things he intended to accomplish. Dorkle brought him a frog, an old shoe, a turtle, and a crayfish.

On the way back, they approached the cabin from a different side. Tobe stopped on the top of a small hill beside a loaf-shaped stack of rocks. From the branches of a scrub oak a dove fluttered to the ground, acting as if injured. "*Coop, coop,*" Dorkle said. The dove stopped pretending and flew back into her tree.

"This is it," Tobe said, looking down at the rectangle of brown rocks. He rolled one over with his foot.

Dorkle looked from the rocks to Tobe and back to the rocks. "Get the green wonder?"

"It's him," Tobe said. He stooped over to replace a stone among the others, scowling and working the muscles of his jaw. "My father told me—he said, 'If you're tough they can't get you.' And that's what I told them all."

Tobe lifted his head, looking down across the pasture toward the ruffle of cottonwoods far away at the big creek. "I don't need anybody, I told them. And after a while, they went away. Well—come on. It's time for chores."

Above the house, to the north, a zigzag of birds scooped across the sky, back and forth like unsettled ashes.

On the days when Tobe went to the store to work, Dorkle jumped and scuffled along beside him, then spent his time sitting on the porch steps patting the dogs that came by, and listening to the old men. They were still arguing.

"Cheepin' and screechin' and making a mess," the one old man said over and over.

The second one, who couldn't hear the birds exactly, had begun to see plenty of them. "I don't know what to make of it," he said. "There does seem to be more than anybody needs."

"It's because the world's different," the third one said.

Bluejays flew down before their feet, cocked their heads and looked with one eye for morsels. Doves sat on the fence rails in pairs and moaned. Mockingbirds, grim and silent, flew with wings that made wheels in the air. The sparrows hopped and flew and hopped and flew.

In the middle of a long tirade about the birds, the old man who was talking stopped. All three turned their heads.

Limping around the corner, dressed in clothes so black with age they seemed green in the sun, came a woman. She looked even older than the old men. Her skirts sifted the dust as she walked. On her head she wore a bright rag wound round, and on top of that a broad hat. From under it her sharp face pointed and her eyes, the color of her dress, looked quickly from side to side.

She walked up the steps beside Dorkle, her skirts making a slipping sound, and something hidden, like bracelets, clattering. The murmuring inside the store stopped when she flung open the screened door.

Presently, she came back out with her purchases clutched to her breast with one hand, and she stirred the dust in the road again as she walked away.

The old men settled back and chewed. "Hoo," one of them said.

Tobe had been inside the store making pyramids of the apples and pears when the old woman came in. He heard the men's voices change.

"Well, howdy, Miz Bonihander," Cooney Mede said. Tobe saw him wink at the other fellows. "Cast any spells lately?"

The others laughed and watched the old woman. She began gathering a few items up into the folds of her skirts.

"How're the goblins?" Cooney Mede said.

"Yeh," Mars Krookford said. "You're supposed to know everything, tell us about these birds. What's the story with all these birds?"

"Right," said Cooney. "We never seen so

many. Screechin' and messin'. They belong to you?"

The old woman whirled her black skirts up to the counter and began removing her selections from them. She spoke for the first time, raising her hand with one bent bony finger up. The hidden bracelets clinked. "If the birds stay, the winter will be easy. If they go, pity your possessions." She closed her lips in a thin pink line like one more wrinkle and said no more.

"Hoo!" Cooney Mede laughed.

Tobe heard the woman's skirts slither past him at the vegetable bin. When the other men had gone, he said to the storekeeper, "Do they really think she can make spells?"

Mr. Stooper shrugged.

"Do you think she's right about the birds? And the winter?"

"Of course not."

But throughout the day one or another person came into the store—sometimes it was one of the old men from the porch—and said, "Them confounded birds. They're getting worse."

"Yep," said someone else.

"Something's going to have to be done."

"We ought to hold a meeting."

And out on the porch, the old men stamped their sticks and flapped their arms and said, "Shoo!" until they grew hoarse. Dorkle listened to them and patted the dogs' heads.

One day before long Tobe said to Dorkle, "Come on. We're going to see somebody."

"Trees the watermelons. Cat?" He tipped his head to one side like a puppy.

"Cat will be all right till we get back—if that's what you said. Hurry now. It's a ways to go." He took up a basket of vegetables from the garden and started toward the trees. Dorkle went leaping after. In the meadow blackbirds and cowbirds blew back and forth, and kill-dees ran on thin legs like wires in and out of the puddles gathered in low places.

"*Dorkle!*" Dorkle said. His eyes closed and the sound rang in the trees.

"Hush your noise," said Tobe.

They saw two gray birds whirl out of the trees, circle and go back. From across the pasture they heard the blackbirds saying it: *dorkle, dorkle.*

They crossed over a low rocky hill covered with catclaw bushes. In them, flocks of tiny finches tinkled.

They came to a sandy path that turned deeper in among the vines and trees. "It's up this way, I think," Tobe said. "I've never exactly been there before."

Dorkle, as ever, discovered worlds at his feet as he traveled: black beetles that stood on their heads; a tarantula who pumped himself up and down on his hairy legs; a dry-looking lizard; thistles that puffed away in his hands.

"Sh," Tobe said. He shifted the basket to his other arm.

There before them, in a cluster of grapevines, was a cottage, squatty and dark but with a clear window on the front side. A row of cats crouched on the stoop watching them through sun-filled eyes.

"*Dorkle!*" The sound cracked the silence. "Cake, fur."

"Well, that did it. We might as well go on up. Isn't anything to be afraid of but I don't see why you can't be quiet some of the time."

He knocked at the door while Dorkle bent over and touched the tops of the cats' heads.

Without the bright rag and the hat on her head, she seemed smaller, Tobe thought when she opened the door. More ordinary. Her thin white hair encircled her head like spider webs.

She gave a little jump backward and said, "Do tell."

"Hi," Tobe said, holding up the basket of vegetables. "My name is—"

"I know who you are," Mrs. Bonihander said. "Don't just stand out there in the breeze."

Tobe and Dorkle entered. The door closed and the old woman's shawls and skirts began to whirl.

"I was about to commence my tea," she said, flapping toward a round black stove. "You're just in time." She tipped an armload of half-grown cats out of a chair. Her hidden jewelry clinked. "Set down," she commanded.

Tobe sat on the chair, warm from the cats, holding the basket on his knees. Dorkle squatted in a corner near a wooden box filled with tumbling, pansy-faced kittens. He put his hands into the box.

"I don't often have company," the old

woman said. She scooped up a portion of her skirts to grasp the teakettle with. "You take lemon or milk?"

Tobe, who had no experience with tea, said, "Both."

"And him?"

"He'll have the same."

Her slippers sang on the floor between the stove and the table. Finally, she seemed to have everything in place.

"Cookies and tumblebugs the deep green," Dorkle said.

Tobe set down the basket. "He doesn't talk too good."

"Makes perfect sense to me," the old woman said. She lifted off the lid of a tin box. "Have a cookie," she said.

Dorkle's eyes grew rounder and bluer. His fingers opened.

"See?" Mrs. Bonihander said. "That's what he wanted. How's your tea?"

"Fine. But . . . his words. They don't make sense."

"People say he was discovered in a tree. Is that right?"

"Yes."

"Well," said Mrs. Bonihander, "it's the same kind of meaning. Words aren't the only language. Now, what's on your mind?"

"My mind?" Tobe tried to pick up the little cup in his fingers.

"What are you doing in this neck of the woods?" Mrs. Bonihander, bent over her tea, smiled. "I know you didn't come on a pure visit." Her lips scooped at the cup.

"Well," Tobe began. Then he began again, "That is, is it true what they say?"

"You might be a little clearer, it seems to me." She handed Dorkle the cookie tin.

"Can somebody really tell things before they happen?"

"Do you think they can?"

Tobe frowned. "Sometimes I know how tomorrow's going to turn out before I get to it."

"But that's not really what you meant."

"Five above the crows. Pickles," Dorkle said contentedly.

"No—it isn't. I really mean, is it true what you told the men about the birds? And the winter?"

She held her lips together tightly and nodded.

"But which way will it turn out?"

"That is up to those bright fellows like Cooney Mede."

"How will we know?"

"You'll know, all right. Keep your eyes and ears open. By the way, do you like cats?"

Surrounded by them at the moment—even a great yellow one that lay among the tea things—Tobe felt he could not say much *against* them.

"Sure—I like cats fine."

"I have a few extras," she said, looking at him hopefully.

"I'd rather have red cattle."

"There's not a world of difference." She searched among her various boxes and corners and brought out a selection of kittens.

"Pan and black the day," Dorkle said. He picked up one gray kitten and looked at it intently in the face.

"We—I guess we'll take that one," Tobe said.

"Only one?" She sat down again and inspected her teacup.

"Do you really have—like they say . . ." Tobe began. "*Powers?*"

"Shoot," Mrs. Bonihander said. "Everybody has *powers*. Some use 'em this way, some that, and some don't ever know they have 'em. Most do the best they can."

Tobe scowled at the big yellow cat next to the sugar bowl.

"Take your mother, now, she—"

"I don't want to hear about it," Tobe said. He pushed his cup away.

"Those that don't want to hear never do."

"What do you mean by that?"

"Life is like a big pickle barrel. And sooner or later everybody falls in it. That's what I call a predicament, don't you?"

"I guess so."

"It's where your mother discovered herself to be, one day. In a predicament."

"She ran away to St. Johns."

"To or away from depends on who's doing the running. You selected to stay here alone. Now you got to show if you have the powers to climb out of the barrel."

As they were leaving she thanked them for

the squash and pole beans and said, squinting in the light, "Look to your provisions."

On the way home, Tobe walked slowly, frowning. Behind him, like a tumbleweed, Dorkle bounded hither and yon, showing the gray kitten the sights of the world.

"We have to work to get ready in case it happens," Tobe told Dorkle when they got home. Dorkle was by then explaining the new kitten to the old three-colored cat.

"We've got to pile up wood. And hay for the cow and the goats. And food." Tobe stood in the room frowning.

"The wide flees."

"The potatoes—my father buried them in the hay. And turnips, too. Corn . . . what there is of it. We can dry the apples."

He began that afternoon chopping extra wood, which Dorkle carried, two pieces at a time, to the barn. The brown cow watched with solemn eyes the shrinking of her space.

The clouds, gray and black, boiled up above the rims of the valley and rumbled. The birds hovered over the meadows, low to the ground. A scarlet cardinal ate sunflower seeds near the hen's fence. Sparrows chattered noisily in the peach tree.

When next Tobe went to work in Mr. Stooper's store, Dorkle sat inside on the bench near the candy counter with his feet drawn up under him. He wore a flannel shirt of Tobe's that made him look like a nomad inside his tent.

The round-bellied stove was lighted. People coming in spread their hands over it and talked of autumn. The three old men moved from the porch and sat on three sides of the stove and spat their tobacco juice into a box of sawdust.

Outside, on the bench, a row of magpies

huddled, looking in through the glass. A pair of roadrunners frantically crossed and recrossed the intersection as if they'd lost something. In the willow, starlings fussed, their voices ringing like metal chimes.

"Look at them fool birds," one old man said. "Cheepin' and screechin'."

"It's the way things are," said the third old man.

Cooney Mede spoke. "We should hold a meeting."

"Right," another fellow said. "Something's got to be done. They're driving the womenfolk loony."

Other men joined them around the stove and before long they were having a meeting. Tobe moved his broom closer.

Dorkle took the gray kitten out of his shirt and let it wobble along the window seat.

"Telling them just to go on away don't seem to work," one man said.

"Nor scarecrows."

"Nor cats."

"My wife says blackbirds are good eating," Homer Oleander said.

"Yeh—and doves, of course."

"And quail."

"And thrushes and sparrows, they say, though I don't recall ever trying them myself."

"Well then," said Cooney Mede, puffing up his chin, "there's your answer. We'll eat them."

"*Dorkle!*" said the small boy on the window seat.

"Perfect," said Mars Krookford. "We'll shoot 'em and eat 'em."

"Excuse me," Tobe said above his broom handle. "But Mrs. Bonihander said—you remember she said if—well, if the birds leave, the winter will come down hard."

"Hoo!" Cooney laughed. "Go on back to your sweeping. We'll see to this."

The Great Hunt of Charley Crossing was organized.

Guns that had been rusting in closets and the bottoms of trunks were brought out and oiled and cocked and clicked and aimed. There weren't many—mostly ancient scatterguns and some small pistols—but Cooney Mede thought they'd do.

Mrs. Oleander wrote out recipes for song-bird fricassee and blackbird pie with mixed vegetables to distribute to her neighbors.

A day was decided upon.

While awaiting it, the people talked of it. From the warm inside of the store the three old men watched the birds sitting on their abandoned bench. "Your time's a-coming," one of them said. He shook his fist at the window.

"Weather like this is fine for hunting," another said.

"Just look there," a lady said who had come to buy ingredients for poultry stuffing. She pointed to a pair of brown wrens who had discovered a way into the store and were flying among the hams and harness leather. "Impertinent creatures."

"Never mind. The day's coming soon."

Tobe listened to the people's plans as he pushed his broom about the store. In the evenings, walking home, he frowned and jammed his hands in his pants pockets.

Beside him, or sometimes behind, leaping and panting and scuffling, traveled the boy. He now wore an outgrown pair of boots that while too small for Tobe were still twice too large for him. In them, he made sounds like herds of hooved animals.

"I think we better do more for the winter," Tobe said.

"Dim the white weeds." Dorkle paused to stuff his pockets with black walnuts. They lay under their trees, bursting from their pods.

"Good idea. Tomorrow, while I cut wood, you gather walnuts."

And he did. By the end of the morning, he came home dragging a gunnysack full. Tobe chopped and thought of red cattle.

The goats paced, nervous and yellow-eyed, in their pen.

On the fence posts and along the wires, clots of small birds sat. The cool wind ruffled their feathers. Sometimes, like brown rag-scraps, they swooped down into the hen's yard and looked for grain. She came rushing out, neck stretched and squawking, to chase them away. Everywhere—in the trees, the meadows, on the rooftop—all day their orchestra played. Dorkle looked up from his work and mocked their songs.

"How do you do that?" Tobe asked. "How do you make all those sounds?" But of course he got no clear answer.

On the special morning, early, before it was light enough to see her, Tobe milked the brown cow. Dorkle fed the goats and the hen. "Sap the high horses," he said.

"Hurry up. They're going to kill the birds today."

"Mumble," Dorkle said, yawning.

"Hurry." Tobe walked with fast steps.

There was something in the morning that seemed different. He couldn't think what it was. The air was sharp and the sky clear.

Just as the sun struck down on them, they reached the edge of the meadow where the hunt was to start, near the center of Charley Crossing. Everybody seemed to be there: the grannies, the ladies, children, the spotted dogs.

And of course, the men with the guns. They sighted along the barrels and pointed them into the air. Their children ran about saying *Bang*.

Some people talked of the weather—"Nice morning." "Yes, still and clear." "Cold, though."—and some talked of cooking—"I think it's best if you brown them first." "Or roasted with giblet gravy."

Tobe was still bothered by the peculiar *tone* of the morning. "What is it?" he wondered aloud.

Dorkle, standing beside him, shivering, said,

"Crow the spoons and candy."

"Oh, you're no help," Tobe said.

Finally, someone decided it was time to begin. The men milled another minute, then spread out along the pasture. Cooney Mede's plan was to scare the birds up and, as they flew this way and that, shoot them in a cross-fire.

The people and the dogs followed behind, tramping over the dew-lit meadow.

The men with guns lifted their feet high and walked cautiously with bent knees. Some carried knapsacks over their shoulders and wore red caps. They held their firearms before their chests, looking fierce.

"*Dorkle!*" Dorkle said, once. The sound rinsed across the meadow, bright like frost.

"Sh!" the people said.

"Hush," said Tobe. "Or you can't come with us."

Dorkle's viola-blue eyes opened and shut. He busied himself examining a small hole in the ground.

The people walked.

And walked, leaving paths in the wet grass.

Tobe stopped. The woman behind bumped him and said, "Oof."

"Listen," he said.

"Listen," the woman said. "Pass it on."

"Pass it on—listen," the next person said.

"Listen. *Listen.*"

Everybody stopped. Except Dorkle who was following a tiny wobbly fieldmouse path.

"Listen!"

There wasn't a sound. The sun ran like gold over the jewelry of the meadow—the dew-tipped leaves, the stalks of goldenrod. The blue sky looked into its miniature pool-mirrors. A few white butterflies dried their wings.

The people turned back the way they had

come, listening, peering into the oaks and cottonwoods, scanning the air, cupping their hands to their ears. At the store they looked in the willow tree. There wasn't a sound. Not a bird.

"Curious," someone ventured.

"Well," said Cooney Mede, puffed up, "we done it. We got rid of them."

"But . . ." said Mrs. Oleander, thinking of her songbird recipes.

That afternoon the gray-and-white clouds rolled up behind the mountains and spilled over. Like big sleepless faces they looked down on Charley Crossing and rumbled. The day grew still and calm and cold. Once in a while a calf bawled across an alfalfa field as if from far away, or a spotted dog barked. The people began hurrying to their barns and haystacks and woodpiles.

Inside the store, the old men drew closer to the stove. "Boy!" one of them shouted, giving the stove a whack with his stick.

Tobe put aside his broom and threw more coal on the fire. "Do you think it'll freeze tonight?" he asked.

"Yes."

"No."

"Possibly, the way the world is and all."

"It's them birds," one old man said. "I don't apprehend how they picked today to disappear."

"It's mighty and peculiar."

"I'm going home early," Tobe said to Mr. Stooper. "There's apples on the tree and things to do."

"Won't they keep?"

"Mrs. Bonihander said, if the birds leave. . . ."

He and Dorkle walked in the still afternoon just as the clouds closed together across the last patch of blue.

"Hurry," Tobe said. "We've got work to do."

Dorkle ran, his boots and shirt and jacket

and pants swirling around him like sails.

Until dark, and even after by the light of a lantern hung on a branch, Tobe picked apples from his tree. He handed them down in small bags to Dorkle, who transferred them to a larger sack which he then dragged to the barn. The brown cow looked over her stall and blew her breath on his hair while he buried the apples under the straw.

As it grew later Dorkle's trips took longer. Tobe sat in the tree, waiting, thinking of the cold and the birds and all the red cattle in the valley. Finally, Dorkle didn't return at all.

Tobe climbed down and went searching. In the barn, his lantern lit the wide moony eyes of the cow, and then the collection of hand-me-downs that was Dorkle in the straw. "Well, a fine help you are." He gathered up the bundle and carried him into the house and, after removing the boots, put him in the bed.

"A fine help you are," he said again. The three-colored cat and the gray kitten climbed up.

Tobe finished his apple picking, then looked in once more on the cow, the two goats who lay close together in a corner of their pen, and the rusty hen. The night turned as sharp as glass—cold, brittle, and still. He looked for the stars but found none.

Before he went to sleep, he twined his hands behind his head and thought of Mrs. Bonihander's prediction.

Pearly and silent the next morning arrived.

"*Dorkle!*" Dorkle shouted, startling Tobe and the two cats straight up out of sleep. He stood at the window looking between his open hands. "Fly the round blue! Troops!" His eyes were dark and wide. His feet stepped up and down.

"Oh my god," Tobe said, standing behind him looking over his head.

During the night, many things had changed. Opposite Dorkle's nose, on the other side of the glass, snow had piled silently on the sill, and frost had laced webs of ice. Beyond, the world seemed white, even the trees and the peaked mountain. White, glittering, frozen.

"Get your clothes on," Tobe said. "All of them."

They stomped a path to the chicken coop and the barn, Tobe in front, Dorkle leaping into his tracks. From inside her house, the old hen peeped out once and withdrew her head. The snow almost covered her door. Dorkle bent down, scooped away the snow, and made noises to her. She clucked dimly.

In the barn, the brown cow lifted her head when they entered and shook her bell. The water in her drinking trough had turned to ice. The wind whistled in the cracks.

For breakfast Tobe scooped up a big bowlful of fresh snow and brought it in. Dorkle looked from it to him and raised his eyebrows. "Braggle?" he said.

"Wait. You'll see." He poured cream and sugar into the snow and stirred it. "My mother, she—. It's called snow cream. Here."

After the first bite Dorkle grinned.

On their way to the store that morning, they passed in an open field a huddled orphanage of red cattle who turned their tails to the wind. Saliva had frozen like ogres' beards on their white chins, and snow lay in the miniature rivulets of their fur.

A little farther on, Tobe stopped. "Look," he said. Beside the path, nearly covered over, lay the body of a red cow, stiff as ice.

"Far in light running."

Just as Tobe was wondering why she hadn't found shelter under the scrub oaks, or warmth with the other cattle, a lump of snow near her belly moved.

"Frogs!" Dorkle said, pointing.

The lump moved again, feebly. "What is

it?" Tobe said. He touched the mound with his boot. Snow fell away from the tiny white head of a calf, ice like ornaments in its curly hair, its eyes frozen shut.

Dorkle dropped to his knees and began brushing away the snow, uncovering the red and white body. When he looked up at Tobe his eyes were wide and blue. "Lap!" he said. "Down in grow falling."

"Come away," Tobe said.

"*Dorkle!*"

"It isn't any use. He'll be dead in a little while."

Dorkle tugged at the calf's head, putting his face down next to its icy pink nose.

"You'll just freeze yourself," Tobe said. "He's too young . . ." He watched Dorkle pulling the calf's leg, rubbing it, brushing the snow from its ears. "Come on now."

Dorkle turned his face up again. From under the brim of his holey knitted cap his eyes seemed astonished. He jumped to his feet.

"Let go," Tobe said, pulling back his hand.

Dorkle's arms whirled. His feet stepped up and down. "Fine, the warm."

"He'll die."

Dorkle shook his head. The cap slid down over his nose. The calf raised his head two inches, then let it fall back.

"You're the stubbornest . . ." Tobe said. "Well, help me clean him off. Don't use your hat—your head'll snap off with the cold."

They turned back the way they'd come, Tobe carrying the calf in his arms like a load of wood. Dorkle walked ahead, looking back often, falling into drifts.

In the barn they lay the calf down near the old brown cow. She rolled her eyes and huffed.

"She won't have anything to do with it," Tobe said. "It isn't hers."

Dorkle pulled the brown cow's ear. She lowered her head and ran out her tongue. She licked the calf's icy face. Dorkle sat down by it and clapped his hands.

"What is it?" Tobe asked Mr. Stooper, later that morning when they finally arrived at the store. Behind the stove, Dorkle had pulled off his boots, poured out the melted snow, and was examining his toes.

"What do you mean?"

"The cold."

"I don't know," Mr. Stooper said, looking out at the silent white road. "These'll be the last," he said, pointing to the fruit and vegetables. "Won't be any more left alive."

"Will it be that bad?"

A few people stamped into the store, but

they were harried and preoccupied. They only warmed their hands at the stove, bought things like shovels and coal oil, and left, looking quickly at the sky.

The three old men came, shaking on their sticks, to sit by the stove and argue over the conditions.

"Never known it colder."

"I have. Lots of times."

"The world has tipped, is what I think. Things are different."

Cooney Mede and a couple of his gang who owned the scatterguns arrived late in the day. "We ought to hold a meeting," Cooney said.

"Going to be the worst winter."

"Some of the cattle have died already."

The men looked grave and rubbed their hands above the stove.

"It's those birds," one man said, finally.

"*Dorkle!*" the yellow-haired boy said,

emerging from behind the stove. "Snow the high bottoms. Sweet." Mr. Stooper reached him down one piece of red-and-white candy from the jar.

Tobe put aside his broom and moved closer to the men.

"Yep," one old man said. "Those birds—it's what I've said all along."

"There was something peculiar."

"Right," Cooney Mede said. He seemed to be thinking. It took a long time. "You remember what old lady Bonihander said... Wait!"

"What is it?"

"Miz Bonihander."

"What?"

"You remember what she said about the birds. And the winter."

"Hoo!" another said. "That's right."

"Then—then she knew all along."

The men paused and looked wonderingly at the stove or their hands.

Tobe adjusted the flue. "You're—you aren't saying she had anything to do with the cold, are you?" he asked. "Or the birds?"

Cooney Mede and his friends lifted their heads and looked significantly at each other. They moved off into a corner and talked and nodded. They bought whatever it was they came for and left, disappearing in whirling snow.

By the end of the day, there were many stories about the cold—of fruit jars exploding on back porches, of livestock endangered, of tree limbs snapping like icicles in the orchards, ducks frozen in the ponds.

"What do you think?" Tobe asked Mr. Stooper. "About the men, about what they were saying? Mrs. Bonihander and the birds and the cold."

Mr. Stooper paused and looked at his shelves. He shrugged. "Some say she's—peculiar. That she *knows* things."

"Does she?"

"Maybe yes, maybe no. You better start home before dark."

"What are they going to do—the men?"

"I don't know. Sometimes it's better just not to get involved," Mr. Stooper said, looking miserable. "It isn't always everybody's business."

By the time they had put on their wraps, and Tobe had tied strips of burlap around Dorkle's legs to keep snow out of his boots, the evening was coming down quickly, and the snowflakes were like white dashes against the gray.

Tobe walked, bent over into the wind, scowling and thinking. Behind him Dorkle leaped from footprint to footprint, pausing every now and then to watch his breath float away from his mouth. "Hurry," Tobe said, "or you'll freeze in one spot like a post."

That night milk frothed and steamed on the red calf's mouth. He leaned against the brown cow on wobbly legs. She seemed pleased—until Tobe moved the two goats into the barn. She and they lowered their heads and eyed each other.

"There's to be a kid, I think," Tobe said, patting the female goat. "Another one, I mean," he added, pushing Dorkle into the hay.

After supper, before he fell asleep, Dorkle sat on the sheepskin rug watching the flames leap inside the isinglass door of the stove. He laughed when the kitten scratched his toes. The sound, like a crackling bird call, ricocheted in the room.

Tobe, with his hands behind his neck, watched him and thought and thought. After the light was out he stood at the window and looked at the frozen, star-white night.

The next morning he was up first—for a

change. "Come on," he said, giving Dorkle a shake. "We've got things to do."

"Grumble?" Dorkle said, rubbing his eyes.

There was some flimsy sunlight now and then, slipping out between two clouds, then retreating, but the day was no warmer. Tobe led the way into the woods toward Mrs. Bonihander's house. They found the way slow and cold going. Limbs from the black walnut trees and the elderberries had broken and twisted onto the path. Where in summer leafy grapevines snaked across the way tunneling the green light, now there were gnarled ropes crushed by the snow and ice, ready to catch their feet.

Whenever he tripped and fell, Dorkle came up laughing with a face full of snow. Tobe would wait a moment, saying, "Watch where you're going or we'll never get there."

But Dorkle seemed to move up and down about as much as forward.

Tobe stopped where the two forks of the way joined into a single path. "Sh!" he said.

They saw how the snow had been trampled by footprints, both coming and going. "Hurry!" Tobe said. They began to run.

He found the snow on Mrs. Bonihander's front stoop also trampled and slushed from many large feet, but when he knocked, she was there quickly to open the door.

"It will be warmer inside," she said. "Unless I stand here holding open this door much longer."

"But—" Tobe said, pointing to the tracks.

Mrs. Bonihander shrugged. Her thin white hair shook. "Nightwalkers," she said. "Fools."

Then Dorkle arrived. "Puff," he said. "Green the—puff—cookies."

"I figured so," Mrs. Bonihander said. "Well, brush off that snow and come in." From the stove she produced three tinkling cups of tea, placing two of them carefully among a nest of cats on the table, the third on the floor near the stove where Dorkle was melting.

"Dreadful weather," she said. She inspected her chair before sitting on it.

"What about the Nightwalkers?" Tobe said.

Mrs. Bonihander tasted her tea. "Lacks something," she said.

"Why did they come? Who are they?"

She laughed. "Hoo! Did you know they wear masks? Knitted face covers. With holes for their eyes." The tea in her cup sloshed when she laughed.

"Who are they?"

"Silliest bunch of grown men you ever saw. And on a night in this weather."

Tobe drank his tea and waited. Dorkle came closer to be near the cookie tin.

"As if I couldn't recognize Madel Krookford's knitting in a mile. And Addie Mede—forever that rib and cable she finds so fancy. I knew them, every one." When she nodded her hair lifted and fell.

"Why?"

She looked into her cup, sadly. "They said, did I bring down this weather on us? Did I send off the birds and bring down the weather?"

Tobe waited.

"Fools and idiots!" she said, stamping her foot. A brindled cat came out from under the table.

"What did you say to them?"

"I told them they were letting in the cold. And I said would they like some tea, the night being chilly and they had so far to go." Mrs. Bonihander chuckled.

"The pity is," she went on, "things will be worse. And it's not but early December."

"Do you have enough food and firewood?"

She looked about the room briefly. Mosaics of fruit jars lined the walls, safe indoors from freezing. "Thank you. More than a-plenty."

"Will they come again?"

She nodded. "I expect so. Things will be worse. Look to your possessions."

"They have to be stopped."

She shook her head. "You won't be able to. People do things, sometimes. Even good people turn fools."

"My father—he said if you're tough, nobody can touch you."

"That's what the thorn bush says." Mrs. Bonihander removed the lid from the cookie tin and set it on the floor. "But the wren don't hear. She builds her nest in it anyway, and sings. Then the snake comes . . . Isn't much a thorn bush can do about a snake."

Tobe stared into his cup.

"That's his *way,* don't you know. Stubborn.

Sticky. The bush, the bird, the snake. It's the way of things."

"That's not the same as this."

"Agreed. The snake don't think he's bad. He does what he feels is right."

"But so did the wren—"

"And the thorn bush."

Tobe shook his head and thought for a second he heard some pieces broken loose inside it, but the noise was only Dorkle rolling spools for the kittens to chase. "What, then?" he asked.

Her eyes brightened. "Will you boys do me a favor?"

"Sure—just tell us."

"Bob," said Dorkle, nodding.

She scuttled around the room until she found an old basket, then began snatching kittens from hither and yon—one from the group on the table, another from behind the stove, two from the woodbox—until the basket was boiling over with them. Her hidden jewelry clinked as she worked.

Tobe's eyes grew almost as wide as Dorkle's.

"They're so young," she said, handing him the basket. "The big ones—well, they can make do."

"But—" Tobe began.

"Dark the jam and under," Dorkle said in awe. He looked into the roiling basket. "Piggles."

"Kittens," Tobe corrected automatically.

As he retraced the way through the woods, stopping often to collect either Dorkle or a tumbled kitten from a snowdrift, he frowned and scowled and thought. "What did she mean," he wondered. " 'The big ones will make do.' What does she know?"

Before long Dorkle had to stand on a chair at the window to see above the snow-drifts. When he went to the barn he walked between white cliffs.

In the barn, he sat down by the brown cow, warmed by her breath and body, and gabbled to her and the red calf and the goats. Tobe came upon them more than once, the animals listening and watching his hands describe adventures in the air.

"Coop the deep inward," he said to Tobe

one day, pointing to the hen's house. "*Boc, boc.*" He made a sound something like hers.

"What is it? I wish you could make sense." Tobe stood with his head drawn down into his collar.

Dorkle pointed from the hen to the barn.

"You want to move her? Is that it?"

Dorkle nodded and grinned. He made flying motions with his arms. "*Boc, boc.*"

"Well—I guess she's not going to run away in this weather . . . not that it'd be much of a loss."

So while Dorkle carried her frozen water dish, Tobe scooped up the rusty hen, who looked about with her head jerking and her comb flapping, and moved her to the barn. There she stood up tall on her yellow toes and eyed the goats and the brown cow and the red calf.

The cold deepened.

Tobe explained how they must use fewer pieces of wood for the fire or it would soon all be gone. They ate the mellow apples and the walnuts and, every day, a potato or a carrot or a turnip. The animals ate the straw. The hen pecked corn. In the evenings Dorkle sat under a blanket near the faintly heated stove and laughed at his seven kittens walking in their milk saucer. The old three-colored cat had taken to sleeping in high places.

Dorkle still trudged behind Tobe to the store, although it was deep going. Nearly every time, they passed new victims of the winter—the bodies of cattle and goats, and once even a coyote who looked as if he had died running. Tobe stopped and frowned and flexed his hands.

Fewer people came to the store. The old men hadn't been seen outside their houses in weeks. For one thing, there was little left to buy. Mr. Stooper's shelves were almost empty and the stove did little good against the cold.

Tobe pushed his broom and looked for things to do.

But one morning when he got there, late because of having lost Dorkle temporarily in a drift, he discovered the front porch of the store stamped and sloshed. Many feet had come in and out. He remembered the morning on Mrs. Bonihander's stoop.

"Bog the ripe clouds. Strawberries," Dorkle said, pointing at the tracks.

"Hush," Tobe said. They entered the store, still rich and full-smelling compared to the outdoors. "Hush, now," he whispered.

Cooney Mede and four or five of his cronies were there, encircling the stove. They had built up the fire until the sides of iron had turned red. They stamped their feet and flailed their arms.

"I think I'll never be warm again," one of them said.

"Thought we'd never make it," said another.

"Especially when Mede took the wrong fork."

"Well," Cooney said, "I've never been there before even in the daylight, much less at night in the snow."

The other men laughed tightly and looked at their gloves.

Tobe got his broom and began sweeping up the tracked snow and mud. Mr. Stooper's mouth seemed drawn like a string purse.

"Where've they been to?" Tobe asked him.

Mr. Stooper shrugged. "Never mind," he said.

"What've they done?"

"Don't ask me. Just go on with your work. There's two crates to open in the storeroom, soon's you warm up a bit. The last of them.

Here, take the boy over this piece of candy."

Tobe frowned and pushed his broom closer to Cooney Mede and Mars Krookford and the others.

"Well," he heard Cooney saying, "the winter'll be gone soon."

"Yep. Should start leaving today."

"She ought to have to pay for all the damage—the cattle and everything."

"Right."

"Her and them birds!" Cooney said.

Tobe dropped his broom. The handle made a loud crack like a shot when it hit the floor. The men jumped.

"Did you say—" Tobe began. "What about *who* and the birds?"

The men looked at him, then each other, then their hands.

"What?" Tobe said.

"I've got chores," one fellow said. He began buttoning up his coat.

"Who are you talking about!" Tobe pulled on Cooney's sleeve.

"Let go," Cooney said. "And mind your own business."

"*Duggle,*" Dorkle said with his mouth full.

The men filed out into the white world.

"Tell me," Tobe asked Mr. Stooper. "Is it Mrs. Bonihander they mean? The Nightwalkers?"

Mr. Stooper looked miserable. He nodded.

"What did they do to her? You have to tell me!"

"They took her away."

"Away? Where? How? Why?"

"Last night, in the Krookfords' old sleigh, they took her to St. Johns and left her. They just got back a while ago." Mr. Stooper sat down on his stool behind the cash box.

"Didn't anybody try to stop them?"

Mr. Stooper lifted his hands with the palms up. "Nobody knew but them. It was secret."

Tobe banged his hand on the counter. The jars jumped and lids rattled. "Cowards!" he said.

"They think she had something to do with all those birds. And the winter. The people's cattle are dying."

"Do you believe it?"

"And before long, there's not going to be anything left in the store. I'm nearly out of coal oil already."

"Well, then, I guess you don't need a stockboy anymore."

"Now wait, I never said that."

"Come on, Dorkle. Get your things on."

"Now . . ." Mr. Stooper began again.

It was easy to follow the tracks to Mrs. Bonihander's house now. There were the hoofprints of the horses, coming and going, and the marks from the sleigh runners. Tobe stopped at the place where the road narrowed too much for the sleigh, where they had turned it around. Beside the path he found a broken jar of spiced peaches. From there, the footprints continued.

"Rub the fly downward," Dorkle said in a small voice. His eyes were wide and blue under his cap.

The door and windows of Mrs. Bonihander's cottage were flung open. Snow had already begun to blow across the sills. Inside was a mess, the pots and pans dumped out on the floor, the teapot spilled, the woodbox overturned, the shelves stripped of their jars, mud and melted snow tracked across the braided rug. The cats had all disappeared.

Tobe stood in the middle of the room opening and closing his mouth. He felt Dorkle's body standing very close to his.

"Dumb the cog lightest."

"You can say that again." Tobe kicked through the papers and broken teacups and scattered spices on the floor. "Here—help me spread out these blankets. She'd be ashamed to think of it looking like this."

In the process of cleaning, Dorkle discovered the cookie tin knocked under a dresser, dented, but with its contents unharmed. "Crackles!" he said, looking from it to Tobe.

"Okay. I don't think she'd mind."

As they were leaving, Tobe found a note tacked to the door. Printed in big, crude letters it said: Suffer Not Witshes to Live in Charley Crossing. Signed, The Nightwalkers. At the bottom, in red, was the word Bewear.

Tobe tore away the note and crumpled it in his pocket. "If I could, I'd explain all this to you," he said to Dorkle.

The winter did not leave with Mrs. Bonihander. It grew worse.

Tobe brooded and studied the white icy view from the window, shifting his head a little when from a distance he heard the sharp cracks of the cottonwood limbs falling to pieces.

Dorkle spent much of his time in the barn, circled by the smells and the animals, including the seven kittens he transported in an apple box with rope tied to it for pulling over the snow.

The hen had adjusted to her new surroundings and laid an egg nearly every morning. The cow gave a thin stream of milk, enough for the red calf and some left over. The goats had their baby. Over it, the father stood yellow-eyed and proud, but his ribs stuck out because there was not enough to eat. He had finished all the harness leather and an old saddle blanket. Above them, along the rafters, the mice stopped and looked down, their eyes pinheads of flint.

One morning, after leaving Dorkle with instructions about the fire, Tobe shook some coins from his money can and floundered toward the store to see if Mr. Stooper had any more coal oil for the lamp.

The day seemed more silent than any ever had. He met not a single creature abroad in the cold, nor saw even the tracks of one. There wasn't a sound of cattle or of spotted dogs or, of course, the birds. The earth seemed as empty of life as the sky. Over the surface of the snow the wind sometimes whirled in small twists, flinging up powdery stings of frost. Blackening branches of cottonwoods twisted up as if in pain like old hands. In the oaks dark clots of mistletoe hung like roosting vultures.

The store was closed and blinded and locked.

No wrinkle of smoke rose from the chimney, no glint of light through the shutter-cracks. Snow lay undisturbed against the door and like deep frosting on the old green bench. Tobe saw a ragged note nailed to the door. He shuddered. But all it said was, Closed: All Out of Everything.

From beneath the porch a thin dog crawled and then stood with its legs apart and head down. When Tobe stepped closer it snarled and sidled away and stopped, panting, leaning against the building.

Across the intersection the other buildings of

Charley Crossing—the community hall, the school, the church—stood as deserted as the store. For a moment, Tobe supposed everyone had left Charley Crossing. Abandoned it. And forgot to tell him they were leaving.

Then he saw first one figure, then two others, step from behind the community hall across the road. Dressed in black and dark gray, with only a slice of their faces showing, they did not seem like any people he could remember. He raised his hand. They stopped, huddled together, and observed him. They did not return his greeting.

Suddenly a stranger in an unfamiliar place, Tobe left the store and walked the other direction in his own tracks. Once he looked back and saw the three black figures still standing at the edge of the hall watching him. He hurried.

After that he never left his place for the

rest of the winter. Sometimes at night he believed he heard people prowling outside or in the wind the sounds of a weeping woman. Sometimes by day he thought he caught glimpses of the three dark figures standing down by the turn of the road, waiting.

The baby goat, small and weak, could not seem to get the hang of walking, and its mother was too hungry herself to provide for it. Tobe, listless and lost in dreams, watched Dorkle make a nursing contraption. Into an old medicine bottle he poured some of the cow's milk, then stoppered it with a rag. The baby goat sucked on the rag. Dorkle held it across his knees when he and the animals visited. The kittens learned to lap from a dish without stepping in it.

"You've got to stop giving them food," Tobe said. "Or there's not going to be anything for us to eat."

Dorkle looked upward from the half-circle of animals. He did not say anything for a change. Under his eyes dark smudges had grown like streaks of coal dust against his skin turned pale and bluish. He seemed to have shrunk inside his collection of rags. At night, in the bed, Tobe could feel how much thinner and lighter his body had become.

The days dragged by, one into the next, gray and still, and the nights came early and deep. Even after the clouds broke apart and the sun returned, pale but blinding, the cold lingered.

But gradually icicles began to form on the eaves of the barn, dripping downward a while at midday, growing, freezing again by evening. Some of the trees shook off their loads of snow and stretched their black arms and fingers.

One morning Tobe discovered the path of a raccoon near the barn. The pawprints were uncertain and dragging but they were a sign.

"I think we're going to make it, Dorkle."

The boy looked up from his place near the cow and smiled. "Drop the time, over."

"I hope so," Tobe said. He stood with his hands in his pockets and looked across his field. In a few places the smashed tops of blackberry brambles now showed through.

In another week, patches of earth, hard and sullen, appeared. Dorkle led the animals and the hen out into the barnyard where they all blinked and walked stiffly.

"I went down to the little creek this morning," Tobe told him. "It's running. And the ice in the pond—it's just a thin layer."

Reluctantly, the winter withdrew.

What it exposed as it left was more of the carcasses of animals caught by it, and the broken limbs of the apple and peach trees, the split and blasted branches of the walnut trees and the cottonwoods. And a peculiar silence.

"Okay," Tobe said one morning. "It's time. Do you think you can make it to the store?"

"Candy?" Dorkle said, searching for the armholes among all the other holes in his coat. "Blang the water matter. Green!"

"We should comb your hair."

"Haggle?" The blue eyes widened.

Tobe laughed—and was surprised by the sound. "Well," he said, running his hand through his own hair, "I doubt that it'll matter. Come on."

They walked through patches of mud still frozen, and thin quilts of snow in the wooded areas. Generally, they could see far across the dipping pastures to the lacey, leafless cottonwoods that bordered the big creek.

"Look!" Tobe said. He stopped and pointed. Under a stand of oaks there huddled a half-dozen red cattle, thin and uncertain, but alive.

Where the snow had disappeared in the

pastures, the grass lay brown and old like the earth.

They approached the store cautiously.

The shutters were open, however, and the door unlocked. They scraped off their boots and entered.

Once again the stove was red-hot, and that coupled with the smells of the place—the leather and the linseed oil on the floor and the bolts of new cloth—and the sights of the bright signs on Mr. Stooper's walls clouded Tobe's eyes and widened Dorkle's.

Only two of the original old men sat by the stove, and there were some others Tobe did not recognize. They turned quietly when they heard the door open. They stared. Their eyes seemed larger and deeper than any Tobe had remembered.

From the other side of his counter Mr. Stooper watched them approach.

"Hello," Tobe said.

"*Dorkle!*" Dorkle said. The sound flung around the angles of the room, reverberating.

"Hush."

"I—I—" Mr. Stooper began. "I'm glad," he said. He shrugged and looked down at the floor. "I was afraid you hadn't—made it."

"It was not so bad." Tobe held himself straight and would not look at the platter of doughnuts in the screened cage.

"Ah," Mr. Stooper said, slumping tiredly onto his stool. "Then you made out better than some."

"Do you need help? Shall I work now?"

Mr. Stooper raised his hands and nodded. "I haven't—yet—any money to pay you."

"It can wait."

"They broke in, you know, near the last. They took everything that was left."

"It doesn't matter—about the money, I mean."

"Well, you know where the broom is."

While Dorkle edged around behind the stove and dried his boots, Tobe pushed the broom. Then it was, when one of the men raised his head, he recognized Cooney Mede. And another, with a deep black beard and sunken eyes, was Mars Krookford, grown older.

They were discussing the spring.

"There's never been a spring like it," one old man said. "Things should be up and growing by now."

"Right," said Cooney in a light, dry voice. "The trees aren't beginning to bud."

"No leaves. No blossoms. That means no fruit."

"The grass—you noticed?"

"Yep. Isn't any."

They fell quiet again, looking down into their hands.

"It's not a proper spring."

"We ought to hold a meeting, I guess."

"And the stillness. Have you noticed it?"

"Yes."

"It's enough to drive you away."

"It's the winter that done it," the second old man said.

"I lay it onto them birds," the first said. "Always have."

The others nodded a little but said nothing.

"Cheepin' and screechin' and . . . all."

"It's next winter will be worse, if there's no planting, no fruit, no hay. What about next winter?"

Mars Krookford seemed to shiver inside his shirt. "Why are the days so still and quiet?"

"That's a stupid question!" Tobe stood beside them holding his broom tightly in his hands. The men turned to look up at him but did not answer. Cooney Mede opened his mouth and ran his tongue over his lips.

"But—" Mars Krookford said, "how did the

birds know to leave? Who warned them?"

"I think I know," Tobe said.

"It was that old woman," Cooney Mede said.

"Mrs. Bonihander? Then why didn't she warn herself about the Nightwalkers?"

The men continued looking from him to their hands. One of the old ones said, "She sent the birds away and brought down the winter."

"How do you know that?" Tobe asked.

"Because . . ." the old man began. His mind drifted.

"The point is," another said, "not then, but the future. What are we going to do about this spring and summer and next harvest? Nothing's coming up to grow."

"What if the birds came back?" Tobe said.

"You can't turn things around."

"Why can't you?"

"It ain't nature."

"You were ready to kill the birds. Was that nature? And running off Mrs. Bonihander, was that?"

"You don't understand," an old man said.

"Hoo!" Cooney Mede said. "How are you going to do it—get the birds to come back, Mr. Smart?"

Tobe looked at his own white knuckles bent around the broom handle. He had a great desire to break it over Cooney's head. "We'll make you a deal," he said.

"*We*? Who—you and that tongue-tied bag of rags?"

"Yes. We get the birds back, you go find Mrs. Bonihander wherever you left her and bring *her* home. And fix up her place again like it was."

"Some say she—they say she has powers," one of the two old men muttered.

"Everybody has *powers*," Tobe said. "Some are just too weak or—" he looked at Cooney who was watching his fingernails "—too mean to use them with any sense."

"You have a lot of sass for a kid," Cooney said.

"Yep," Tobe said. "You're right. Lately I've had time to develop it." He leaned his broom against a table and sat down in the vacant chair by the stove. He crossed his arms and stretched out his legs and crossed them, too. "Well?" he said. "You better get started for St. Johns."

"You haven't proved your half. Do you promise?" Cooney said, but he and Mars Krookford began buttoning their coats.

"What good would a promise be to you?"

"And—even if they come back, how do we know things will be all right again?"

Tobe stood up. His eyes were on a level with Cooney's. "You don't," he said. "Come on, Dorkle. Everybody's got things to do."

"Green the willow, yellow," Dorkle said, looking around for his mittens.

Outside, they walked down the double track of the long road, between two barren fields of stubble and black orchards. The sun shone down cold and shrill. Tobe waited now and then while Dorkle inspected holes and rocks and the undersides of last autumn's fallen leaves.

"Can you do it?"

Dorkle stopped leaping and tipped his head to one side. "Cattle?"

"*Birds.*" Tobe laughed. "Birds, you dope."

He watched the viola-blue eyes close and the boy's head tip back, topped by the winter's meringue of yellow hair. The sound he made, startling and bright and ringing, traveled like light across the meadows.

From a distance, Tobe thought he heard a faint, tinkling reply: *dorkle!* When he looked he believed he saw—then was sure of it—a handful of shapes, like pieces of soot, flying straight up into the sky.